Pegasus Princesses

AQUA'S SPLASH

Pegasus Princesses

AQUA'S SPLASH

Emily Bliss

illustrated by **Sydney Hanson**

BLOOMSBURY
CHILDREN'S BOOKS
NEW YORK LONDON OXFORD NEW DELHI SYDNEY

BLOOMSBURY CHILDREN'S BOOKS
Bloomsbury Publishing Inc., part of Bloomsbury Publishing Plc
1385 Broadway, New York, NY 10018

BLOOMSBURY, BLOOMSBURY CHILDREN'S BOOKS, and the Diana logo
are trademarks of Bloomsbury Publishing Plc

First published in the United States of America in September 2021
by Bloomsbury Children's Books
www.bloomsbury.com

Bloomsbury books may be purchased for business or promotional use. For information on
bulk purchases please contact Macmillan Corporate and Premium Sales Department at
specialmarkets@macmillan.com

Library of Congress Cataloging-in-Publication Data
available upon request
ISBN 978-1-5476-0684-9 (paperback) • ISBN 978-1-5476-0685-6 (hardcover)
ISBN 978-1-5476-0686-3 (e-book)

Book design by Jessie Gang and John Candell
Typeset by Westchester Publishing Services
Printed and bound in the U.S.A.
2 4 6 8 10 9 7 5 3 1 (paperback)
2 4 6 8 10 9 7 5 3 1 (hardcover)

To find out more about our authors and books visit www.bloomsbury.com
and sign up for our newsletters.

For Phoenix and Lynx

Pegasus Princesses
AQUA'S SPLASH

Chapter One

On a warm Saturday morning, Clara Griffin slid on her belly across her blue living-room carpet, paddling with her arms. Her black hair was in a tight ponytail. She wore pink goggles, a pair of teal flippers, and her favorite bathing suit— lime green with a ruffle and a shiny picture of a violet mermaid on the front. Clara pinched her nose—just the way she did when she jumped into a swimming pool—and did two somersaults. She pulled a large hardcover book off the coffee table and held it out in front of her like a kickboard. Then she kicked and pretended to blow bubbles.

Clara's younger sister, Miranda, lay nearby on their family's yellow corduroy living room couch and looked at an animal encyclopedia. She turned a page, stared for a few seconds at the photographs, and raised her eyebrows. "What in the world are these weird-looking animals?" she whispered. "M-m-m-" she began, trying to sound out a word at the top of the page. Then she looked at Clara. "Will you please read this to me?"

Clara lifted her head and pretended to gasp for breath. "I'll read it to you as soon as it's adult swim," she said. Adult swim was Clara and Miranda's least favorite time at their neighborhood pool because all the kids had to get out of the water for fifteen minutes. Clara kicked for a few more seconds. She made a loud, high-pitched noise meant to sound like a lifeguard's whistle. And then she paddled over to the couch.

Clara hoisted herself up onto the cushions and sat next to her sister. She took off her flippers and goggles. She pretended to wrap herself in a towel. And then she looked down at the encyclopedia.

"Those animals are called moles," Clara

said, reading the word at the top of the page. For a few seconds, she and Miranda studied the photographs of mouse-sized

creatures with gray fur, pink noses, stubby tails, small squinty eyes, and giant front paws that looked like pink flippers.

"What does it say about them?" Miranda asked.

Clara read out loud: "Moles live mostly underground. They use their large front paws to dig tunnels. While many people believe moles are blind, it turns out that's a myth. Moles can't see color, and it's true they can't see very well. But they can see light and movement."

"Thanks," Miranda said, sitting up and grabbing her sketch pad and pencil case from the coffee table.

"No problem," Clara said.

Miranda opened her pencil case and paused. "I think I've made a plan for the morning," she said. "First I'm going to sketch a mole. After that I'm going to practice my ukulele. Next I'm going to reorganize my sock drawer. And then I'm going to pack up my swimming bag for when we go to the pool later. If I have time, I might also do the math flashcards I made for myself."

Clara thought about what to do next. She felt finished with pretending to swim. She wasn't in the mood for drawing realistic pictures or practicing the ukulele. She had no plans to ever reorganize her sock drawer. She had already packed her swimming bag. And even though she liked math, she hated flashcards. She glanced down at the photographs of the moles and smiled at their huge, flipper-like paws. The paws were so large and strange that moles looked to Clara like they ought to be magical creatures. And then Clara had an idea. She leaped off the couch. She twirled in a circle and hopped from one foot to the other with excitement.

"Let me guess," Miranda said. "Did you just have an idea for a creative project?"

"Yes!" Clara sang out. "I'm going to make a family of magic, flying moles. Then I'm going to build a magic tunnel world under my bed out of old paper towel tubes. I'll call it the Mole Realm! And I'm going to do it right now so it will be finished by the time we go to the pool."

"That sounds really neat," Miranda said. "Have fun making the Mole Realm. I'd love to see it when you're finished."

Clara galloped across the living room, bounded up the stairs two at a time, skipped down the hallway, and burst into her bedroom.

The first thing Clara needed was the modeling clay her grandparents had given her on their last visit. She raced over to her desk and opened the bottom drawer. Underneath five rocks she had found on a hike, sea shells from her last trip to the beach, a few interesting twigs, acorns she had painted gold, a pinecone, and a long strand of braided yarn, Clara found a package of peach-colored modeling clay still in its plastic wrapper.

She sat down on her bed and opened the modeling clay. She began to sculpt a family of magic moles with giant flipper-paws, fairy wings, and unicorn horns. As she paused to consider adding triangular stegosaurus spikes to the moles' backs, she heard a humming noise. At first, Clara ignored the sound, thinking it was Miranda practicing her ukulele. But as the humming grew louder and louder, Clara realized it wasn't coming from the living room, or even Miranda's room down the hall. Instead, it was coming from under her bed!

Clara slid onto the floor. She reached

under her bed and pulled out a shoebox she had decorated with paint and sequins. She opened the box, and inside it was just one item: a large silver feather.

Glittery light shot up and down the feather's spine as it hummed louder and louder.

Clara grinned from ear to ear. The feather had been a gift from the pegasus princesses—eight royal pegasus sisters who ruled over the Wing Realm, a magical world where all the creatures had wings. Just a few days before, Clara had visited the Wing Realm for the first time. There she had made friends with silver Princess Mist, teal Princess Aqua, white Princess Snow, green Princess Stitch, pink Princess Rosie, peach Princess Flip, black Princess Star, and lavender Princess Dash.

Clara had learned that each princess had a unique power: Mist could turn invisible; Aqua could breathe underwater and make magic bubbles; Snow could freeze water and create winter weather; Stitch could use magic to sew, knit, weave, and crochet almost anything; Rosie, whose real name was Rosetta, could speak and understand any language; Flip could do a magical somersault that would turn her into any animal; Star had extraordinary senses of sight, smell, taste, and hearing; and Dash could instantly transport herself anywhere in the Wing Realm. Each pegasus princess had a special, magical tiara with a gemstone design that matched her powers. The pegasus princesses lived with their pet cat, Lucinda, in Feather Palace, a giant silver castle that hovered in the sky above a forest.

At the end of Clara's visit to the Wing Realm, the pegasus princesses had told her she could use the silver feather to come visit them again any time. All she had to do was run, holding the feather, into the woods surrounding her family's house. Then a light-green armchair with wings would appear and take her to Feather Palace. Mist had also told Clara that if the pegasus princesses ever wanted to invite her to the Wing Realm for a special occasion, they would make the feather shimmer and hum—just the way it was shimmering and humming right then!

Clara couldn't wait to visit the Wing Realm and the pegasus princesses again. She picked up the feather, stood up, and raced to her bedroom door. But before she could open it, she looked down and realized she was still wearing her bathing suit. Clara scanned the floor of her bedroom for clothes she could quickly put on. Amid piles of crayons, building toys, books, and stuffed animals, Clara found a crumpled pair of pink pants and a rolled-up turquoise T-shirt she had been using as a pillow for her stuffed alligator. She pulled on the pants and T-shirt over her bathing suit. She pushed her feet, without socks, into her lime-green canvas sneakers. And then she put the feather in her back pocket.

Clara raced out of her room, down the hall, down the stairs, and into the kitchen, where her father was humming along to music as he cut a head of broccoli into florets. "I'm going outside to play in the woods. I'll be back soon," Clara said. Time in the human world froze while she visited the Wing Realm, meaning that even if she was there for hours, her father would only think she had been gone for a few minutes.

"Sounds good," her father said. "Just be back in time to go to the pool." He whistled along with a trumpet solo and began to peel a carrot.

Clara pulled open the kitchen's screen door and leaped outside. She hopped along the slate stepping-stones that led across her backyard and skipped into the forest. For a second, she paused and closed her eyes. She breathed in the smells of moss and pine needles and felt the warmth of the sun against her face and shoulders. Clara opened her eyes and grinned. She pulled

the feather from her back pocket and, holding it gently in her hands, ran down a hill, jumped across a tiny creek, and sprinted to a small clearing near a giant pine tree.

As soon as Clara saw the clearing, a comet of glittery green light swirled above a bed of pine needles. The light flashed. And then, ten feet in front of Clara, there appeared a green velvet armchair with two silver-feathered wings on its back. The wings fluttered. The chair spun on one of its legs. And then it hopped toward Clara. When it was right next to her, Clara giggled and sat down. "Please take me to the Wing Realm," she said.

The chair lurched forward. Its wings began to flap. Clara tightened her grip on the chair's arms as it sailed into the air and landed on top of a tree. It leaped again and paused on the roof of Clara's family's house. And then, flapping its wings even more, it soared upward and began to spin, faster and faster. Everything went pitch black. And then the chair landed with a clatter on a tile floor.

Chapter Two

The front hall of Feather Palace looked just the way Clara remembered it from her first visit. Gauzy curtains fluttered in the breeze over feather-shaped windows. Portraits of the eight pegasus princesses and Lucinda hung on magenta walls. Light danced and glittered on the shiny black marble floors. On stone pedestals, pegasus statues reared up, wings outstretched. Pegasus fountains spouted rainbow water. Eight empty thrones—each with a color and design that matched one of the pegasus princesses— were arranged in a horseshoe shape in the center of the room. Clara grinned when she saw that Lucinda's small silver sofa, with its back shaped like a cat head, was pushed right next to Aqua's teal throne.

At first Clara thought she was alone in the front hall. But then she heard a voice above her call out, "At the count of three, start kicking." Clara looked up. Just below the front hall's vaulted ceiling, all eight pegasus princesses were flying in a giant circle. They were all wearing large teal flippers strapped to their hooves. And they

were so immersed in their swimming lesson they didn't notice Clara had arrived.

Aqua swished her tail and said, "One. Two. Three. Kick!"

The pegasus princesses began to kick their front and back legs as they flew.

"Those kicks look great," Aqua said. "Now, start paddling with your wings like this." She swept her wings from front to back.

Mist, Stitch, Rosie, Star, and Dash all began to paddle their wings as they kicked. But Snow jabbed a flipper into her wing, stopped kicking, and then flew sideways as she tried to paddle. Flip swept her wings from back to front and bolted backward, flailing her legs in every direction. After a few seconds, Flip and Snow crashed into each other.

"Oops! Sorry!" Flip said to Snow.

"That was at least half my fault," Snow said, sighing. "I'm sorry too."

Flip groaned in frustration. "Every time I try to paddle, it's a disaster," she said.

Snow shook her head and snorted. "I feel so frustrated," she said. "I need to take a break from this swimming lesson."

"Wait!" Aqua called out, hurrying over to Flip and Snow. "You can't give up now. I know you can learn to swim. You just need to keep trying."

Flip and Snow glared at Aqua.

"I'm trying my hardest," Snow said. "Right now, it's just not working."

"I'm trying my hardest too," Flip said. "And I'm getting so frustrated that I need to do something else for a little while. Otherwise, I feel like I might explode!"

Aqua's face looked panicked. "I know you're both trying your hardest. And I really appreciate it. But you can't quit now. The Merthday Splash is *this afternoon*. If you can't swim by the time the celebration begins, the whole thing will be ruined," she said. "Could you please try again? I really think you've almost got it."

Flip groaned and flared her nostrils. "I promise I will keep trying," she said. "But not right now."

Snow nodded. "I'm willing to try swimming one more time before the Merthday

Splash," she said. "But first I'm taking a break with Flip."

Aqua bit her lip and flattened her ears with worry as Flip and Snow dived down to their thrones. They snorted and frowned as they pushed off their flippers and shoved them onto the floor. And then, as they looked back up at each other, they both noticed Clara sitting in the green armchair opposite them. Flip and Snow's eyes widened in surprise. Their frowns turned into enormous grins. And then they both leaped off their thrones and galloped over to Clara.

"Clara is here!" Flip called out.

"We're so happy to see you," Snow said, trotting in an excited circle around

Clara's chair. "Welcome back to Feather Palace."

"I'm very happy to see you too," Clara said, laughing.

Mist, Aqua, Stitch, Rosie, Star, and Dash all looked down from just below the ceiling. They grinned and whinnied with delight. And then they swooped down, landed in a circle around Clara, and pushed off their flippers.

"I'm thrilled you're here," Aqua said, flapping her wings with excitement. "You've arrived just in time."

"We were hoping you would be able to come," Star gushed.

"I was crossing my hooves you'd be able to join us," Stitch said.

"Welcome back, human friend," Mist said with twinkling eyes.

Dash and Rosie swished their tales and reared up.

"I'm so glad to be here," Clara said. "Thank you for inviting me back to the Wing Realm."

"I can't wait to tell you what we're doing today," Aqua gushed, twirling in a circle on one of her rear hooves. "It's going to be amazing and perfect! I've helped to organize the first ever Merthday Splash. It will be a special celebration for the baby merfairies, who will hatch this afternoon. I've spent weeks making plans with the merfairies and teaching my sisters to swim so we can all dive into

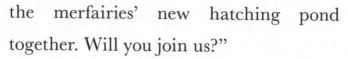

the merfairies' new hatching pond together. Will you join us?"

"I would love to," Clara said, standing up and jumping with excitement. "But I do have one question. What is a merfairy?"

Aqua's eyes widened in disbelief. "You don't have merfairies in Gardenview, New Jersey?" Gardenview, New Jersey, was the name of the town where Clara's family lived.

"We have pet canaries and libraries in Gardenview. But we definitely don't have merfairies," she said.

The pegasus princesses' eyes widened in surprise. "The human world must be such a strange place," Rosie whispered.

"I can't even imagine it," Dash whispered back.

"Well," Aqua said, "a merfairy is a magical creature that's half fairy and half fish. They're kind of like mermaids, but they're smaller and have wings. Every year, the baby merfairies hatch inside the merfairies' underwater castle, and we have never been able to watch. But this year will be different and extra special. The merfairies dug a special hatching pool on Heart Island in the Sky Sea so my sisters and I can watch the eggs hatch and hold the first ever Merthday Splash."

"That sounds amazing," Clara said.

"I'm so glad you can join us," Aqua said. "I was thinking I'd leave for the Sky Sea in just a few minutes. I spent all morning painting decorations for the Merthday Splash, and I want to make sure they're perfectly arranged around the hatching pool. Would you like to come help me?"

"I'd love to," Clara said.

Just then a voice purred, "Wait! Don't go quite yet!"

Clara smiled and turned around to see Lucinda flying into the front hall. She flapped her silver-feathered wings as she soared in a circle around a chandelier. She did two somersaults in the air. And she then landed right on Clara's head. Clara giggled as the cat swished her soft silver tail across Clara's face and batted Clara's ponytail with her front paws.

"Will you please, please, please play a guessing game with me before you go to Heart Island with Aqua?" Lucinda asked.

"Of course," Clara said.

"How about if I guess how old you are in three guesses?" Lucinda asked.

"Okay," Clara said.

Lucinda jumped off Clara's head and hovered right in front of Clara's face. The cat touched her cool, wet nose to Clara's, and Clara smiled as Lucinda's whiskers tickled her cheeks. "My first guess," Lucinda said slowly, "is 119."

Clara shook her head.

"Rats!" Lucinda said. "Am I close?"

"Well," Clara said. "Not really."

"Hmm," Lucinda said. She fluttered her

wings and turned upside down in the air. "In that case, my next guess is 643."

Clara shook her head.

"Double rats!" Lucinda said, righting herself and landing on the floor. "This time I'll get it. I'm absolutely sure of it." She squeezed her eyes closed and purred loudly for a few seconds. "It just came to me," she said, opening her eyes. "You are 3,742 years old."

Clara shook her head. "I'm eight," she said.

"Triple rats!" Lucinda said. She flicked her tail back and forth. "Well, I don't want to be a sore loser. Thank you so much for playing."

Clara reached down and scratched

Lucinda behind the ears. The cat purred and twitched her tail.

Aqua smiled at Clara and Lucinda. "I think it's about time to go to the Sky Sea," Aqua said. "Are you ready?"

"I sure am," Clara said, standing.

"In that case, climb on up," Aqua said as she kneeled. Clara swung her leg over Aqua's back and gripped the pegasus' curly teal mane.

Aqua stood up and turned to her sisters. "I'll meet you at Heart Island in an hour. Stitch, would you be willing to bring the flippers?"

"Of course," Stitch said.

Then Aqua looked at Flip and Snow. "Why don't you two meet me by the hatching pool just a little early for one final swimming lesson?"

Flip sighed. "Fine," she said.

Snow nodded. "I know how much the Merthday Splash means to you," she said. "I'll try one more time."

"Fantastic," Aqua said. "I'm sure you'll be able to learn to swim. I just know you will. Especially because we absolutely cannot let anything ruin the Merthday Splash."

When Aqua wasn't looking, Clara saw Flip and Snow both sigh, roll their eyes, and flare their nostrils.

Aqua turned to Lucinda. "Do you want to come to the Sky Sea with Clara and me?"

Lucinda blinked her large, emerald eyes. She looked at Aqua. And then she looked at

Flip and Snow, who were both frowning. "I'll come with Flip and Snow," Lucinda said. "They seem like they could use some cheering up. Plus, I want to play a guessing game with Rosie right now. She promised I could try to guess her favorite flower. I'm still deciding whether to start by guessing violets or buttercups."

Clara giggled. "Are you going to guess roses?" she asked.

"Definitely not," Lucinda said. "There is no way that's the answer."

Clara and Rosie looked at each other and smiled. Rosie winked, and Clara winked back.

"I'll see you all soon," Aqua called out as she turned and galloped toward the front double doors of Feather Palace. The doors magically flung open to reveal a clear blue sky and a sea of green treetops below. Aqua leaped out of the palace and soared into the air.

Chapter Three

As Aqua climbed higher and higher in the sky, Clara turned her head for a moment and admired Feather Palace. Sunlight sparkled on the pegasuses' castle, which looked like two silver wings surrounded by towers and turrets.

"I can't wait to show you the Sky Sea," Aqua said. "And I'm thrilled you'll be part

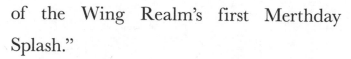

of the Wing Realm's first Merthday Splash."

"Thank you so much for inviting me and including me," Clara said. "It sounds like you and the merfairies worked hard to plan it."

"We sure did," Aqua said proudly. "I want it to be absolutely perfect. But," she continued, her voice lowering with worry, "I'm getting nervous Flip and Snow won't learn to swim in time. And if they can't swim, they can't dive to the bottom of the pool to sing while we watch the eggs hatch. And that will ruin the entire Merthday Splash."

"I can definitely understand how you feel," Clara said. "My seventh birthday party was at a skating rink and—" Clara paused. "Do you have ice skating in the Wing Realm?"

Aqua laughed. "Good question," she said. "We do. Snow especially loves to skate, and she can even do all kinds of turns and spins in the air. But I can't make it across a frozen pond without falling over at least ten times. Usually I end up using my magic to make a giant bubble that I can get inside. That way I can just slide across the ice, and I don't have to worry about trying to skate. Anyway," Aqua said, "keep telling me about your birthday party."

"Well," Clara said, remembering the party. "I invited my four best friends— Neela, Ada, Min, and Natalee—to my party. I had a plan that the five of us were going to spend the entire time ice skating without taking any breaks. I didn't even want us to stop skating to eat cupcakes or open presents. But do you know what happened? It turned out that Natalee and Neela had never skated before. They tried to learn, and I tried to teach them. But they both got so tired and frustrated that they decided to sit in the cafe, drink hot chocolate, and play checkers for the whole rest of the party. At first, I was sure my birthday was ruined. I even asked my mother if we could just go home. But then, as Min, Ada, and I skated and waved to Natalee and Neela each time we passed them, I realized we could all still have fun, even if the party didn't go exactly the way I planned it."

"If I had been at your birthday party, I would have wanted to drink hot chocolate with Natalee and Neela," Aqua said, laughing.

Clara smiled. And then, gently, she added, "It might be that Flip and Snow feel the same way about swimming that you feel about ice skating. Instead of trying to rush them to learn to swim by this afternoon, I wonder if there might be a different way they could participate in the Merthday Splash."

"Huh," Aqua said, sounding uncertain. "I hadn't considered that. I guess I need to think about it a little more." She sighed.

And then in a bright voice she said, "The good news is we're almost to the Sky Sea Gateway."

Aqua flew over a stretch of forest and then soared upward, higher and higher. "Do you see that cloud that's exactly the same color as I am?" Aqua asked. Sure enough, in the distance Clara saw a teal cloud. "That's the entrance," Aqua said, flying even faster before she glided downward. She landed in the center of the cloud, right next to an archway made of rose-, peach-, and watermelon-colored shells. The air under the archway shimmered and glittered, and warm salty air wafted through it.

Aqua kneeled. "Why don't you climb off

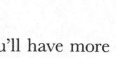

here?" she said. "I think you'll have more fun with this next part if you're on your own two feet."

Clara slid off Aqua. She expected the cloud to feel spongy and bouncy under her feet, but instead, to her surprise, it felt like it was made of hard-packed sand.

Aqua looked at Clara. "Are you ready?" she asked with a playful smile.

"Yes," Clara said.

"Follow me," Aqua said. She turned toward the shell archway. She paused for a moment. And then she leaped through it. To Clara's surprise, Aqua disappeared into the shimmering air!

Clara stood for a moment and looked at the archway. The air beneath it swirled and glittered as a gust of warm salty air riffled through Clara's ponytail. She inhaled and smiled. And then she turned, counted out loud to three, and jumped through the archway.

For a brief moment, everything went pitch black. And then Clara found herself standing next to Aqua on a long stretch of glittery bright pink sand. Mauve crabs with pale wings skittered and darted near Clara's feet. Magenta sea oats and fuchsia beach grass swayed in the breeze on a nearby row of high sand dunes. The strong smell of salt water hung in the air. Clara heard birds calling and waves crashing.

"Welcome to the Sky Sea," Aqua said. "It's my favorite part of the Wing Realm."

"I can see why," Clara said. "It's beautiful here."

"It sure is," Aqua said. "And you haven't even seen the sea or Heart Island yet. Come this way."

Aqua galloped across the sand and pebbles to the row of sand dunes. Clara skipped after her, enjoying the feeling of her sneakers shuffling in the sand. Clara and Aqua scaled the side of a dune and paused at the top. Just in front of them, a pink sandy beach gave way to a turquoise ocean with frothy waves that lapped the shore. Long-legged sea birds with cotton-candy- and grapefruit-colored feathers waded in the surf, swooped into the waves, and cawed in the air. Green and orange fish with gold wings burst from the water, flew a few feet, and dived back into the waves. A winged purple octopus rocketed out of the sea with a splash, waved its tentacles at Aqua and Clara, and sang out, "Good morning!" before it flopped back into the sea.

Aqua laughed. "That octopus is my good friend Octavia. She gave me several jars of her black ink to use to paint all the Merthday Splash decorations."

Clara nodded. She had read in Miranda's animal encyclopedia that octopuses could shoot out black ink.

"Do you see that island?" Aqua asked, squinting at the horizon.

Clara followed Aqua's gaze. Sure enough, amid the waves, she spotted a heart-shaped pink island. "Yes," Clara said.

"That's Heart Island," Aqua explained. "The fastest way to get there is to fly. But the way that's the most fun to get there is to swim. I told the merfairies I'd stop by their underwater palace to get them on the way to the island. Would you like to swim there with me?"

Before Clara could respond, Aqua's face fell. "Oh, I just realized I've been so worried about whether Flip and Snow can swim that I completely forgot to ask if you can." She blushed and grimaced. "Do you happen to know how?"

"I sure do," Clara said. "And I'm even wearing my bathing suit under my clothes."

Relief and joy washed over Aqua's face. "Wonderful," she said.

Then Clara paused. "The only thing is, humans can't breathe underwater."

"That's not a problem," Aqua said, with a wink. "Most pegasuses can't breathe underwater either. But I can because that's one of my magical powers. Just tell me when you're ready to go in."

Clara peeled off her shirt, her pants, and her shoes. "I'm ready," she said, hopping up and down in her lime-green bathing suit.

"Watch this," Aqua said, grinning with excitement. The gemstone water droplet design on her tiara sparkled. And then a clear bubble the size of a beach ball appeared in front of Clara. For a few seconds, it hovered in the air, spinning and shining in the sun. Then, in a burst of teal light, Clara's head was inside the bubble! "As long as you're wearing that magic bubble, you'll be able to breathe and talk and see underwater," Aqua said.

"That's amazing. Thank you," Clara said. She reached up her hands and touched the bubble. It felt cool and soft, like a cross between glass and silk. "I can't wait to try it."

Aqua reared up and barreled down the dune, galloped across the sand, and crashed into the waves.

"The water is perfect today," she called out to Clara.

Clara sat down in the sand and slid to the bottom of the dune. Then she ran across the warm soft sand and stepped into the surf. Aqua was right: the water was cool and refreshing. Clara ran through the waves to her pegasus friend, and the two jumped and splashed deeper and deeper into the sea. When the water was as high as Clara's neck, Aqua turned to Clara and said, "On the count of three, let's dive underwater."

Clara nodded.

"One. Two. Three!" Aqua and Clara said together before they both plunged below the waves.

Chapter Four

Clara blinked and looked all around her. Sand, pebbles, and shells covered the sea floor. She took a long deep breath. And then another. It was true: with the magic bubble on her head, she could see and breathe underwater.

Aqua swam over to Clara, paddling with her wings and kicking with her legs. And then she did two flips.

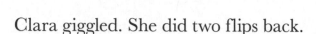

Clara giggled. She did two flips back.

"Kelp Castle—that's the name of the merfairies' palace—is just a little farther this way," Aqua said, swimming deeper into the sea.

"I can't wait to see it," Clara said, paddling alongside Aqua.

Aqua glanced over at Clara and said, "Sometimes I like to invent my own swimming strokes."

"You do?" Clara said. "Me too! That's my favorite thing to do at the pool with my sister."

Aqua flashed a playful grin. "I call this one the Banana-Eating Kangaroo in a Hurry," she said. Then, she made a frantic jumping motion with her hind legs as she used her front legs to pretend to cram a banana into her mouth.

Clara laughed so hard she had to stop swimming for a moment. And then she began doing the Banana-Eating Kangaroo in a Hurry too. After a few seconds, she said, "Now I have one. I call this the Sleepy Octopus Doing Yoga." Then she yawned and fluttered her eyelids as she pretended her arms and legs were undulating tentacles doing downward dog and warrior one—two yoga poses she had learned in her gym class at school.

"I love it!" Aqua said, yawning and snoring as she pretended her legs and wings were flailing, yoga-doing tentacles.

They pretended to be sleepy octopus

yogis for a few more seconds. Then Clara noticed thick clumps of rainbow-colored seaweed growing in the sand. As they swam, the seaweed grew longer and longer, and the clumps thicker and thicker. Soon they came to what looked like a seaweed forest. Red, orange, yellow, green, blue, and purple strands of seaweed, each as tall as a tree, swayed and fluttered in the current. "To get to Kelp Castle, we have to swim through here," Aqua said, kicking and paddling right into the seaweed.

Clara followed her, smiling at the feeling of the soft, slippery seaweed brushing against her legs and arms as she kicked and paddled. Soon Aqua and Clara swam into a clearing. Hundreds of tiny bubbles, glowing with yellow-orange light, floated in the water, illuminating an elaborate shell-shaped palace. The castle, which was about the size of Clara and Miranda's dollhouse, was made entirely of tiny seashells and rainbow-colored seaweed that had been braided, woven, and knit together to form archways, domes, towers, turrets, bridges, and walkways.

"Wow," Clara whispered. "That is an amazing palace."

"Welcome to Kelp Castle," Aqua said. "Can you believe the merfairies made it? Stitch offered to help them weave and braid the seaweed, but they said they wanted to do it all by themselves."

"Doesn't the seaweed ever tear or break?" Clara asked.

"Almost never," Aqua said. "The magic seaweed in the Sky Sea is incredibly strong."

For a few seconds, Clara stared in wonder at Kelp Castle.

"Are you ready to meet the merfairies?" Aqua asked.

"Yes," Clara said.

Aqua cleared her throat. And then, in a loud voice, she sang out, "We're here!"

After a few seconds, three creatures burst out the front door of Kelp Castle. Each looked to Clara like a colorful, doll-sized mermaid with shiny silver wings. They each held in their hands a basket made of seaweed and an instrument made of a large seashell with seaweed strings. Aqua grinned. "Clara, allow me to introduce you to my good friends, the merfairies."

"I'm Mira," said a merfairy with a scarlet tail, indigo skin, and short kelly-green hair.

"I'm Myrna," said a merfairy with a yellow tail, lime skin, and wavy peacock-blue hair said.

"And I'm Moira," said a merfairy with a robin's-egg-blue tail, fuchsia skin, and straight lavender hair said.

Then, all together, Mira, Myrna, and Moira said, "It's absolutely wonderful to meet you."

"I'm thrilled to meet you too," Clara said.

"Aqua has told us all about you," Mira said.

"And we're delighted you can join us for the Wing Realm's very first Merthday Splash," Myrna said.

Moira nodded. "We've spent the

morning playing our shellophones and practicing the special songs we wrote for the occasion."

"And we each just checked our eggs," Mira said, smiling and holding up her basket. "Every one of them is ready to hatch this afternoon. We've packed them up in our baskets and we're ready to bring them to the hatching pool on Heart Island."

Aqua smiled. "Wonderful. My sisters and I are excited to help you welcome your babies to the Wing Realm."

"Let's swim to Heart Island now," Mira said. "I want to get there in time for one last shellophone practice session. I keep playing wrong notes!"

Aqua, Clara, Moira, Mira, and Myrna

swam together around the back of Kelp Castle and through a thick stretch of rainbow seaweed forest. When they came out on the other side, the water was shallow enough that Clara and Aqua could stand with their heads above the water. And right in front of them, sparkling in the sun, was Heart Island.

Aqua and Clara walked to the shore as Moira, Mira, and Myrna burst out of the water and flew alongside them. Heart Island was about the size of a tennis court. At its center, surrounded by pink sand, was a large heart-shaped pool. Arranged along the edges of the pool were six white canvases. And sitting in the sand next to the pool was a large glass jar of black ink.

Moira, Mira, and Myrna flew over to the pool and put their baskets of eggs down. Then Mira said, "We're going to practice our hatching song one last time. It's the song that tells the babies it's time to come out of their eggs, and we want it to be perfect."

Aqua nodded. "That sounds great," she said. "Flip and Snow will be here any minute now for one last swimming lesson."

The three merfairies flew to the other side of the island and began singing and playing their shellophones.

Aqua looked at Clara. "I don't think you need your head bubble anymore," she said. The water droplet design on her tiara sparkled, and the bubble vanished.

"Thank you," Clara said.

"No problem," Aqua said. "Want to come see the decorations I painted while we wait for Flip and Snow?"

"I'd love to," Clara said. "Painting is one of my favorite activities."

"Me too," Aqua said as they walked across the sand to the pool.

Clara spent several seconds admiring Aqua's paintings. Each was a combination

of bold black stripes and big, elaborate black swirls. "Your pictures really are beautiful," she said.

"Thank you," Aqua said. "I used my tail as a paintbrush. I dip it right in that jar of octopus ink and paint away."

Clara smiled. "Maybe I should try using my hair as a paintbrush sometime."

"Great idea," Aqua said, admiring Clara's wet ponytail.

Clara kneeled next to the pool and looked down. She thought the water looked like it was about as deep as the diving area at her neighborhood pool.

Just then she heard the sound of wings beating in the distance. She turned and saw Flip, Snow, and Lucinda flying straight toward Heart Island. The three landed by the pool, skidding in the sand. Flip and Snow smiled at Clara, but she could see in their eyes that both pegasuses still felt frustrated and annoyed.

"Hello," Lucinda purred, swishing her tail. She looked at Clara and said, "You absolutely won't believe this, but Princess Rosie's favorite flower is a rose. A rose! I was shocked. She gave me eight guesses, and then she told me the answer."

Clara giggled and said, "Oh, Lucinda." She bent over and scratched behind the cat's ears and petted the soft fur on her back.

Aqua looked at her sisters. "Thank you so much for coming early. Let's get started right away on your swimming lesson," she said. "Maybe it will help if we practice in the water instead of the air."

Flip sighed. "All right," she groaned.

"We've agreed to try our hardest," Snow said.

"But," Flip said, "we have also agreed we can't promise you we'll be able to swim before the Merthday Splash."

"And we don't like it when you put so much pressure on us," Snow added.

Before Aqua could respond, Lucinda suddenly yawned five times. Her eyelids began to flutter. "Flying over here was exhausting," Lucinda said. She yawned four more times. "I may need to take a quick catnap." Rocking back and forth and yawning, Lucinda ambled over to a particularly bright patch of sunlight next to the jar of octopus ink. With her eyes already closed, she flopped down into the sand and rolled onto her back. As she began to snore, she twitched her tail—and knocked the entire jar of ink into the hatching pool. Clara, Aqua, Flip, and Snow gasped as the water in the pool turned jet black.

Chapter Five

"Oh no," Flip said, staring at the black, opaque water.

"What will we do?" Snow asked.

"This is a catastrophe," Aqua said as her eyes filled with tears. "We have no choice but to cancel the Merthday Splash."

Mira, Myrna, and Moira stopped singing and playing their shellophones. They rushed over to the hatching pool. For a few seconds they hovered above the pitch-black water. And then Mira said, "Oh dear."

"I think we'd better just cancel the Merthday Splash," Myrna said.

"The eggs can hatch in Kelp Castle the way they always have," Myrna said.

Mira and Moira nodded. "We'll just hold the Merthday Splash next year," Moira said.

Tears streamed down Aqua's cheeks. "I know you're right," she sniffled. "I just feel so very disappointed. I guess I should fly back to Feather Palace and tell the others not to bother coming after all."

Clara stared at the water. She took a long, deep breath. "Before you go," she said slowly, "why don't we all think together for a minute about whether there is any way to save the Merthday Splash."

Mira, Myrna, Moira, Aqua, Flip, and Snow nodded. For several seconds, they all stared at the pool with furrowed brows.

Flip sighed. "I'm trying my hardest, and I can't think of any creative solutions," she said.

Snow shook her head. "Me neither. I didn't want to have to learn to swim today, but I definitely didn't want the Merthday Splash to be canceled."

"I can't think of anything either," Aqua said.

Clara looked for a moment at the water droplet design on Aqua's tiara, the snowflake design on Snow's tiara, and the spiral design on Flip's tiara. She thought for a minute about the strong seaweed the merfairies used to build Kelp Castle. And then, suddenly, Clara had an idea. Her eyes widened. A grin spread across her face. She hopped up and down. And then she twirled in a circle. "I have a plan to save the Merthday Splash," she said.

"Really?" Aqua asked, looking hopeful.

"I will do anything to help," Snow said.

"Me, too," Flip said, nodding.

"Count us in," Myrna said. Mira and Moira nodded.

"If we all work together, I bet we can do it," Clara said. She turned to Mira, Myrna, and Moira. "Do you think you could braid a rope out of rainbow seaweed?"

"Of course," Mira said.

"Easily," Moira said.

"How long should it be?" Myrna asked.

Clara looked at the hatching pool. "About six times as tall as I am."

"We'll be back with a seaweed rope in just a minute," Mira said.

The three merfairies turned, flew to the Sky Sea, and plunged in. A few seconds later, they returned carrying piles of rainbow seaweed in their arms. As they hovered in the air, Mira quickly used her fingers to braid the seaweed as Moira and Myrna handed her strands.

"It's ready now," Myrna announced,

holding up a long, tightly braided seaweed rope that was tied on both ends.

"Excellent," Clara said. "The next step is to fly with it over the hatching pool and let each end dip into the water so it makes a rainbow shape."

"A rainbow shape?" Myrna said, raising her eyebrows. Moira, Myrna, and Mira looked at each other and shrugged. Then they flew over to the hatching pool, each carrying a section of the rope. They let the rope's ends dangle into the water.

"Maybe lower the ends of the rope just a little more into the pool," Clara said.

"Sure thing," Mira said, and the three merfairies all flew downward so the rope went deeper into the black water.

"That's perfect," Clara called out. "Excellent work!" Next, she turned to Snow. "Do you think you could use your magic to freeze the hatching pool water?"

Snow cocked her head in confusion. She stared for a few seconds at Moira, Mira, and Myrna, hovering in the air and holding the rope. And then her face brightened. She reared up and called out, "I know what you're thinking." Snow turned to the hatching pool. The gemstone snowflakes on her tiara sparkled. And then, in a flash of light, the pond turned into a giant piece of black ice.

"Wonderful," Clara said. "Now we can get rid of that inky water." She turned to Snow, Flip, and Aqua. "Could you help the merfairies use the seaweed rope as a handle to pull the ice out of the nest? I was thinking you could drop it out in the Sky Sea to melt."

"What a great idea," Aqua said.

"I'd be thrilled to help," Snow said.

"Me too," Flip said.

The three pegasus princesses flew over to the merfairies. They each grabbed a section of the seaweed rope in their mouths.

"Start flying up at the count of three," Clara said. "One. Two. Three!"

Clara sucked in her breath. For a few seconds, Aqua, Snow, Flip, Mira, Moira, and Myrna were all pulling upward on the rope as hard as they could, and nothing was happening. But then the giant chunk of ice began to slowly slide upward. "It's working!" Clara called out. "You can do it!"

The ice kept sliding upward while the merfairies and the pegasus princesses pulled as hard as they could. And then, with a loud scraping noise, they were all suddenly up in the air holding the biggest, darkest piece of ice Clara had ever seen. Together, they flew toward the horizon out over the Sky Sea, and when Clara could barely see them, they dropped the ice. Then, they flew as fast as they could back to Heart Island.

"You did it," Clara said. "Good job!"

Aqua, Snow, and Flip panted. "I think that was the hardest I've ever worked," Aqua said.

"I've never lifted anything that heavy," Snow said.

"Phew!" Flip said.

Mira, Moira, and Myrna looked uncertainly at each other. And then they looked at Clara.

"Thank you for getting the inky water out," Mira said slowly. "But, it's just that—"

"Well, the thing is, I don't want to disappoint you, but—" Myrna began.

"What we're trying to say is that, once we dug that pool, it took us three months to get enough water in it," Moira said.

"We spent all day, every day filling up buckets in the Sky Sea and dumping them out in the hatching pool," Mira said.

"I still think we may need to cancel the Merthday Splash," Myrna said. "Even if we all got buckets and started pouring water into the hatching pool right away, there isn't enough time to fill it up."

Chapter Six

Aqua's face fell as she stared at the empty hatching pool.

Snow gazed down at her hooves.

Flip looked like she might start crying.

But Clara smiled. "I have an idea to fill up the hatching pool quickly," she said. "It's the part of my plan I'm the least sure will work. But let's try it!"

Snow, Aqua, Flip, Moira, Mira, and Myrna all nodded hopefully.

Clara turned to Flip. "Is there any chance you could turn yourself into a mole?" she asked.

"I've never turned into a mole before," Flip said. "And I cannot wait to see what this next part of your plan is." The gemstone spiral design on Flip's tiara sparkled. She flapped her wings, flew up into the air, and did a somersault. In a bright flash of light, a peach-colored mole with tiny wings appeared in the sand.

"Hello!" Flip squeaked in a high voice.

Clara, Snow, Aqua, and the merfairies giggled. "Hello," Clara responded.

"I can barely see you," Flip squeaked,

squinting and waddling toward Clara. Clara giggled. She reached down and picked up Flip in her hands. Then she held the mole right in front of her face.

"There you are," Flip squeaked, pushing her nose against Clara's.

"Luckily, for this next part, you won't need to see well," Clara said, laughing. "But you will need to get wet."

"I'm fine with water as long as I don't have to swim," Flip squeaked.

"Excellent," Clara said. She turned to Aqua. "Could you possibly make Flip a head bubble so she can breathe under water?"

"Of course," Aqua said. The gemstone waterdrop design on her tiara sparkled. A bubble appeared in front of Flip's head. It spun in a circle. And then, in a flash of light, Flip's head was inside it.

"Now you're ready," Clara said, cupping Flip gently in her hands. "What we need you to do is wade into the Sky Sea and then dig an underground tunnel from the sea floor to the side of the hatching pool," Clara said. "That way, the sea water will flow through the tunnel and fill up the pool."

"I can certainly do that," Flip squeaked, turning and waddling across the sand and into the Sky Sea. With her flipper-like front paws, she began to dig downward, disappearing quickly into her own hole.

Clara, Aqua, Snow, Mira, Moira, and Myrna all watched the empty pool. Clara took four more deep breaths before she spied two peach flipper-paws poking out from a tiny hole on the inside of the nest. Water began to run out of the hole as Flip kept digging. Aqua reared up and whinnied with excitement. "It's working!" she said, as more and more water gushed from the hole and into the hatching pool.

After just a few more seconds, Flip crawled all the way out of her tunnel and climbed up the side of the merfairy nest to the sand. "Did it work?" she squeakcd.

"Yes!" Clara, Snow, Aqua, Mira, Moira, and Myrna all called out at once.

"Hooray!" Flip squeaked. She did an excited dance on her back feet and front flipper-paws. And then she flapped her wings, did a somersault in the air, and turned back into a pegasus. Flip looked down into the hatching pool, which was filling with water.

Aqua reared up and whinnied. "It worked," she said. "The pool will be full by the time the rest of my sisters get here. Now we can hold the Merthday Splash."

"Excellent job, everyone," Clara said, smiling. "We did it!"

"Thank you for such a creative idea," Aqua said.

"Thank you for working together and

being willing to try out my plan," Clara said.

For several minutes, Clara, the pegasus princesses, and the merfairies watched as water flowed into the hatching pool.

Then Clara heard wings beating the air. She turned. Mist, Star, Dash, Stitch, and Rosie were soaring above the Sky Sea, flying straight toward them.

"Hello!" Mist called out as the rest of the pegasus princesses landed in the sand on Heart Island.

Stitch held in her mouth a mesh bag bulging with teal flippers. She dropped the bag and exclaimed, "As soon as we put on our flippers and get our magic head bubbles, we'll be ready to dive into the hatching pool for the Merthday Splash."

Mist, Rosie, Stitch, Star, and Dash all looked expectantly at Flip and Snow.

"So," Dash said, "did you learn to swim?"

"How was your final swimming lesson?" Rosie asked.

"Will you be able to join us?" Star asked.

"Well—" Flip began, frowning and looking down at her shiny, peach hooves.

"Actually—" Snow started, and she let out a long, anxious sigh.

Aqua cleared her throat. She looked at Mist, Rosie, Stitch, Star, and Dash. And she said, "It turns out Flip and Snow were too busy saving the Merthday Splash to have a final swimming lesson." Aqua told her sisters the story of how Lucinda knocked the octopus ink into the hatching pool and then Clara, Aqua, Flip, Snow, Mira, Moira, and Myrna all worked together to fill the pool with new, clear water.

"Wow," Star said, looking at Flip and Snow, "you really did help save the Merthday Splash."

Rosie, Mist, Stitch, and Dash nodded in agreement.

Aqua winked at Clara. Then she said, "I've realized the Merthday Splash can still be great even if it doesn't go exactly the way I imagined it would. Making sure everyone feels comfortable and can participate in their own way is more important than exactly following the plans we made."

Flip and Snow looked at each other. Their eyes widened and they smiled hopefully.

"I was thinking," Aqua said, "that I could make big magic bubbles that would fit over Snow and Flip's whole bodies—the same kind of magic bubble I wear when I can't ice skate. That way, they wouldn't have to swim at all. And they can still join us."

"That would be perfect," Flip said, as relief washed over her face.

"Thank you, Aqua," Snow said. "That's a fantastic solution."

Aqua looked down at her hooves. "I'm sorry I put so much pressure on you to learn to swim before you were ready. I wanted the Merthday Splash to be perfect. But I had just one idea in my head about what a perfect Merthday Splash would look like. I'm really sorry. I want you to know I'm happy for you to be part of the celebration in a way that works for each of you."

"I accept your apology," Flip said.

"Me too," Snow said.

Aqua smiled and sighed with relief. She turned to Stitch, Rosie, Dash, Star, and Mist. "Let's put on our flippers!"

Aqua, Stitch, Rosie, Dash, Mist, and Star reared up and whinnied with excitement. They pushed their hooves into their flippers. Clara giggled. She thought her pegasus friends looked like they had teal duck feet.

"Now it's time for the magic bubbles," Aqua said. The water droplet design on her tiara glittered and sparkled. Beach-ball-sized bubbles appeared in front of Clara, Stitch, Rosie, Dash, Mist, and Star. The six bubbles spun in the air and shimmered in the sun. And then, in six bursts of light, the bubbles were on Stitch's, Rosie's, Dash's, Mist's, Star's, and Clara's heads.

Aqua looked at Flip and Snow. She smiled warmly. "I'm so glad you're joining us in this way," she said. The water droplet design on her tiara sparkled again. Two

giant pegasus-sized bubbles appeared in front of Flip and Snow. They spun and shimmered. In two bursts of light, Flip and Snow's entire bodies were inside the bubbles. Flip giggled as she began to float up into the air. "The way the bubbles work is you just imagine in your head what direction you want to go in, and then they float that way," Aqua said.

Snow smiled and furrowed her brow. Suddenly, her bubble shot upward. She laughed. "This is a thousand times easier than swimming," she said.

"It sure is," Flip said, floating even higher into the air.

"Fantastic," Aqua said.

"Should we wake up Lucinda so she can join us?" Clara asked.

All eight pegasus princesses shook their heads. "Lucinda absolutely hates water," Star explained.

"It's because she's a cat," Dash said, shrugging.

"She'll be happiest if she just takes a nice long catnap in the sun," Mist said.

"We're ready for the Merthday Splash!" Aqua announced, rearing up with excitement.

"So are we," Mira said.

Mira, Moira, and Myrna flew over to their baskets and put the handles over their shoulders so they could still use both hands to play their shellophones. Then they flew right above the hatching pool. They looked at each other and smiled. Moira said, "A one and a two and a one, two, three, four." The three merfairies began to strum and sing as they flew down into the pool.

Chapter Seven

C lara and the pegasus princesses smiled excitedly at each other. Clara, Mist, Aqua, Stitch, Rosie, Star, and Dash walked to the edge of the pool. Flip and Snow glided over in their bubbles. And they all plunged in.

Underwater, the pool echoed with the merfairies' shellophone music. Clara kicked

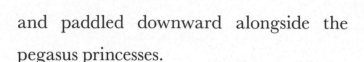

and paddled downward alongside the pegasus princesses.

When they got to the bottom, they found a large, heart-shaped floor covered in layers of folded blankets knit and crocheted from rainbow seaweed. The merfairies sat in the center of the seaweed blankets and sang while Clara and the pegasus princesses gathered in a circle around them. Mira, Moira, and Myrna carefully put their eggs, which had shells with a rainbow swirl design, down on the blanket. Then they picked up their shellophones and strummed as they sang, "Little merfairies, come out today. Little merfairies, it's time to play." Clara and the pegasus princesses

listened for a few seconds. And then they all joined in the singing.

Clara gasped in wonder and delight as cracks began to form in the eggs. The cracks grew bigger and bigger. Tiny fins and arms began to poke from the eggs. Soon, six bald merfairy heads popped out from the shells. And then they pushed all the way out of the eggs and swam up to Mira, Myrna, and Moira.

"Mama?" said a baby merfairy with a green tail and blue skin said.

"Goo! Goo!" said a baby merfairy with an indigo tail and orange skin said.

"Gah! Gah!" said a baby merfairy with a red tail and violet skin said.

Moira, Mira, and Myrna all laughed

and stopped playing their shellophones. They beamed with joy.

"Welcome to the world, little merfairies," Mira said.

"We're so glad you're here," Myrna said.

Moira looked at Clara and the pegasus princesses. "Thank you so much for coming to the first Merthday Splash," she said. "It has meant so much to us for you to be here."

Myrna nodded. "Now it's time for us to take the babies back to Kelp Castle. We built an entire nursery for them. There arc seaweed hammocks for them to sleep in and all kinds of rattles and toys we made from shells and seaweed."

"Thank you for including us in such a special occasion," Aqua said.

Clara, the pegasus princesses, and the merfairies all smiled at each other.

Then Myrna said, "This way, little merfairies!" She, Moira, and Mira swam upward. Clara giggled as the baby merfairies watched for a moment and then swam in a perfect line after their mothers.

Aqua, Stitch, Rosie, Flip, Snow, Star, Dash, Mist, and Clara smiled at each other for a few seconds. "That was amazing," Dash said.

"I hope we can do this every year," Snow said.

"Maybe we'll even have learned how to swim by then," Flip said.

"But if you haven't, it's completely okay," Aqua said.

Clara and the eight pegasus princesses swam to the top of the hatching pool. When they had all climbed out onto the sand, the water droplet design on Aqua's tiara sparkled, and all the bubbles disappeared.

"After all that excitement, I think it's time for some sunbathing," Mist said.

"And there's no better place for rolling around in the sand than Heart Island," Flip said, nodding.

Snow laughed and began to roll around in the sand. Dash, Star, and Mist quickly followed.

Clara giggled as she watched her pegasus friends. And then she felt her stomach

rumbling. She was ready for lunch. And she also felt ready to finish making the Mole Realm under her bed and go to the pool with Miranda and her father.

"I wish I could join you for an afternoon of sunbathing," Clara said, "but I think it's time for me to go back to the human world."

Aqua smiled at Clara. "No problem at all," she said. "I'll take you back to the beach to get your clothes and your magic feather."

"Thank you," Clara said. She glanced over at Lucinda, who was still sleeping. She smiled at the cat, skipped over to her, and whispered, "Goodbye. I'll see you very soon," into her ear.

Lucinda purred, opened one eye, smiled at Clara, and then rolled onto her side and let out a loud snore. Clara giggled and skipped over to Aqua.

Aqua kneeled, and Clara climbed onto her back.

"Goodbye!" Stitch said. "Please come back soon!"

"We'll invite you back as soon as possible," Star said, winking at Clara.

"Thank you for all your help," Flip said.

Snow nodded. "Your creative solution saved the Merthday Splash. Thank you so very much," she said.

"It was my pleasure to spend the day with you," Clara said. "Thank you for having me!"

As Clara waved, Aqua flapped her wings and lifted up into the sky.

Aqua soared above the Sky Sea and flew back to the beach. She landed on the sand dune next to Clara's clothes and shoes. Clara pulled her turquoise T-shirt over her head and slid her legs into her pink pants. She pushed her feet into her shoes. And then she fished the magic silver feather from her back pocket.

She looked over at Aqua. "Thank you again for including me in the Merthday Splash," she said.

"And thank you so much for coming," Aqua said. "You saved the day!"

Clara held the feather in both hands. "Take me home, please," she said.

Clara felt the feather whisk her up into the air. She began to spin as she rose upward higher and higher.

Everything went pitch black, and then Clara found herself sitting in a patch of moss in the woods near her house. For a moment, she sat and smiled. She stood up and pushed the feather into the back pocket of her pants. And that's when she noticed something else was in her pocket. She pushed her hand in and pulled out a neck-lace. The chain was made of woven sea-weed. And hanging on it was a sparkling pink-and-teal-striped shell. Clara smiled. She tied the necklace around her neck. And then she skipped home, ready to eat lunch, make mole tunnels, and swim with her sister.

Don't miss the first high-flying adventure!

Turn the page for a peek . . .

In the library of Feather Palace, Princess Mist, a silver pegasus, flew slowly along the top shelf of books. Right behind her, Lucinda, a silver cat with wings, purred and practiced doing somersaults in the air.

"Where could it be?" Mist asked, hovering for a few seconds in front of a shelf and then gliding forward to the next row of books. "This is where we keep the magic cookbooks. But I don't see it anywhere."

Lucinda twitched her tail. "How about if we play a guessing game while you're looking?" she asked. Then she flipped upside down and, with her paws sticking up toward the ceiling, flew in figure eights around Mist's hooves.

Mist laughed. "I promise I'll play a guessing game with you after I find this book. I've been wanting to host a cloud maze party for my sisters for months. But I can only do it if I know how to make—" Mist's eyes widened as she read the title *Magic Maze Potions* on the spine of a thick

red book. "Here it is!" Mist exclaimed. "Finally!" With her mouth, she pulled the book off the shelf.

Mist flew in an excited circle around a chandelier. She did a flip in the air. And then she swooped down to the floor and placed the book on a wooden desk next to a wing-shaped reading lamp with a rainbow flame. A second later, Lucinda landed with a thud on the desktop, right next to the book.

"Now can we play a guessing game?" Lucinda asked, looking up at Mist with large green eyes. "Please?"

"I promise we'll play one," Mist said. "But let's look up the recipe first."

Lucinda frowned with disappointment.

"How about if you help me turn the pages?" Mist asked, smiling at the cat.

Lucinda purred with delight and swished her tail. Then she used her paw to flip the book open to the table of contents. Mist and Lucinda leaned over the page. Mist began to read the names of the maze potions out loud: "Swirling Rainbow Maze Potion, page 3. Yodeling Corn Maze Potion, page 4. Underwater Coral Reef Maze Potion, page 5. Glowing Yarn Maze Potion, page 6. Blooming Flower Maze Potion, page 7. Glitter Garden Maze Potion, page 8." Then her eyes widened and she grinned. "Giant Floating Cloud Maze Party Potion, page 9," she read, flapping her wings with excitement.

Emily Bliss, also the author of the Unicorn Princesses series, lives with her winged cat in a house surrounded by woods. From her living room window, she can see silver feathers and green flying armchairs. Like Clara Griffin, she knows pegasuses are real.

Sydney Hanson was raised in Minnesota alongside numerous pets and brothers. She is the illustrator of the Unicorn Princesses series and the picture books *Next to You, Escargot*, and *A Book for Escargot*, among many others. Sydney lives in Los Angeles.

www.sydwiki.tumblr.com